D0473766

Emily Saves the World

A Random House PICTUREBACK® Book

Random House New York

Thomas the Tank Engine & Friends™

CREATED BY BRITT ALLCROFT

Based on The Railway Series by The Reverend W Awdry.
© 2015 Gullane (Thomas) LLC.
Thomas the Tank Engine & Friends and Thomas & Friends are trademarks of Gullane (Thomas) Limited.
HIT and the HIT Entertainment logo are trademarks of HIT Entertainment Limited.
All rights reserved. Published in the United States by Random House Children's Books, a division of Random House LLC, 1745 Broadway,
New York, NY 10019, and in Canada by Random House of Canada Limited, Toronto, Penguin Random House Companies. Pictureback,
Random House, and the Random House colophon are registered trademarks of Random House LLC.

ISBN 978-0-553-50870-3

randomhousekids.com   www.thomasandfriends.com

MANUFACTURED IN CHINA 10 9 8 7 6 5 4 3 2

One sunny day on the Island of Sodor, the engines were talking about some of the exciting deliveries they had made. Duncan had delivered a really big elephant statue. Rheneas had hauled a huge dinosaur skeleton. Gordon had once carried the Queen!

"Wow!" Emily exclaimed. She was pulling a load of sand—definitely not exciting.

When Emily arrived at Brendam Docks, her friend Thomas could see that she was sad.

"What's wrong?" he asked.

"Oh, I've never delivered anything exciting," Emily peeped. How she wished she had!

The next day, Sir Topham Hatt sent Emily to collect a Special.
"Probably more sand," Emily said with a sigh. But it wasn't more sand. . . .
"Bust my buffers!" Emily peeped when she saw her delivery. It was a giant model of the world for the Animal Park! Emily couldn't wait to show the other engines. She chuffed off with excitement.

But there were no engines anywhere along the line. Emily
finally saw Gordon up ahead in Maron Station, but he left before
she arrived. Emily wanted *someone* to see her exciting delivery.
She chugged ahead as fast as her wheels could carry her.

But it was too fast! *BUFF! BOING!* The globe
bounced loose and rolled away.
Emily had no idea that her Special was missing.

Then Emily saw Thomas. "Hello, Thomas!" she said happily. "If you want to see an exciting load, look at this. Isn't it great?"

"Ummm, what do you mean?" Thomas asked, confused. "There's nothing on your flatbeds."

"Oh, no—I must have lost it!" Emily peeped in shock. "I'd better find it, or I'll never get another exciting delivery again!" And off she chuffed.

Down the line, Thomas and Annie were chuckling about Emily's invisible delivery, when . . .

"We might want to hurry it along a bit!" Clarabel suddenly peeped.

"Why?" Thomas asked.

"BECAUSE THERE'S A GIANT GLOBE HEADING RIGHT FOR US!" Clarabel whistled loudly.

Thomas pulled into a siding, and the spinning world kept rolling down the tracks.

"Come back!" Emily called.

The globe rolled all the way to Brendam Docks! Salty tried to stop it. Emily tried to stop it. But the globe spun away—right into the water!

Luckily, Captain was there to push it to the dock, where Cranky picked it up and placed it safely on Emily's flatbed.

"Thanks, Cranky! And thank you, too, Captain!" Emily called as she puffed away.

"My, my, Emily. You are *very* late," said Sir Topham Hatt, when Emily arrived at the Animal Park with the globe safely in tow.

"I'm sorry, Sir," Emily peeped. "I just wanted everyone to see my exciting delivery."

"You certainly did cause confusion and delay. But at least you got here in the end," Sir Topham Hatt replied.

At last, the giant globe was in its proper place for everyone to see.

"Well, Emily," said Thomas as he pulled up next to her. "I think you managed to make that the most exciting delivery ever!"

"Maybe a little bit *too* exciting, Thomas!" Emily said with a laugh.

Thomas smiled at his friend Emily, and then he laughed, too.

"Of course not," Marion said, a little embarrassed. "There aren't any dinosaurs around nowadays."

"That's why I'm building a Dinosaur Park," the Earl replied. "So people can see what these amazing creatures looked like!"

"I can tell them!" Marion said. "They looked big—very, VERY big. And a little bit scary, too!"

And so it had—just a day late. Samson had gotten lost and had spent the night in a quarry before arriving at the castle.

"Here are the models for my Dinosaur Park," the Earl said.

"Dinosaur Park?" Marion peeped.

"Don't be frightened," the Earl said. "They're not real!"

Stephen, Millie, and Marion hid in the castle.

"It's the dinosaurs!" Marion gasped. "I can hear them breathing!"

"That sounds like a steam engine," Stephen said.

"Yay!" someone shouted.

"It's the Earl!" Marion whistled. "Do you think the dinosaurs got him?"

"He sounds happy to me," Millie replied.

"My Special Delivery has arrived!" the Earl called.

Meanwhile, at the castle, Millie and Stephen were still waiting for the Earl's Special Delivery.

But all they saw was Marion hurrying toward them. "That's not it," Stephen said.

"Help!" Marion called. "Dinosaurs are chasing me!"

"She's right!" Millie peeped in fright. "They're coming up the hill now!"

When she looked again, Marion saw *lots* of dinosaurs.
"EEEKKK!!" she screamed, shutting her eyes and backing
away along the track. When she opened her eyes, the dinosaurs
were still coming after her. Marion screamed again and hurried
toward Ulfstead Castle.

After Thomas rolled away, Marion heard another engine coming along. When she looked up, she saw—

"Dinosaurs!" Marion gasped. "Wake up, Marion! You're dreaming again!"

Marion couldn't believe it. She tapped herself with her shovel to be sure she wasn't sleeping.

The next day, Marion told Thomas that she'd seen real,
live dinosaurs on the track the night before.

"But dinosaurs don't exist anymore," Thomas peeped.

"I know," Marion said. "Dinosaurs lived millions of years ago, long before
railways or digging were even invented."

"It must have been a bad dream," Thomas told her.

That night, Marion was asleep when something woke her. She thought she heard an engine on the line. But when she looked, she saw . . . a dinosaur!

"Impossible!" Marion shrieked, covering her face. "It's just a dream!"

But when she looked again, she saw *more* dinosaurs!

"Go away, dinosaurs! Go away, dream!" Marion cried. And then they *were* gone. Marion was quite relieved.

At Ulfstead Castle, Millie and Stephen told Thomas that they were expecting an important shipment from the mainland.

"We don't know what it is," said Millie, "but it's something very big!"

Thomas wondered what it could be.

One day, Marion was clearing a site for some new sheds when Thomas stopped by.

"Oh! Hello!" she said in surprise. "I didn't hear you sneaking up . . . in front of me!"

"You're funny," Thomas said, laughing. "Let me know if you dig up anything exciting, like more dinosaur bones."

Thomas puffed away with a delivery for the Earl of Sodor.

One morning on the Island of Sodor, Marion was digging at the clay pits. Wherever there was a digging job, that was where you'd find Marion!

She was very proud that she had helped uncover the dinosaur skeleton that now stood outside Knapford Town Hall. "Millions of years old, and I dug it up!" she said.

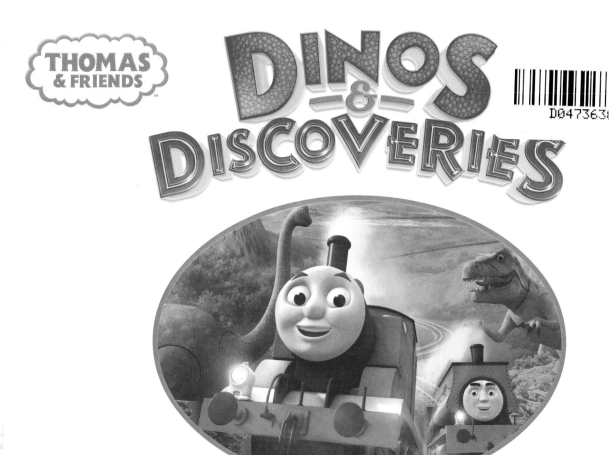

THOMAS & FRIENDS™

DINOS & DISCOVERIES

A Random House PICTUREBACK® Book

Random House New York

Thomas the Tank Engine & Friends™

CREATED BY BRITT ALLCROFT

Based on The Railway Series by The Reverend W Awdry.
© 2015 Gullane (Thomas) LLC.
Thomas the Tank Engine & Friends and Thomas & Friends are trademarks of Gullane (Thomas) Limited.
HIT and the HIT Entertainment logo are trademarks of HIT Entertainment Limited.
All rights reserved. Published in the United States by Random House Children's Books, a division of Random House LLC, 1745 Broadway, New York, NY 10019, and in Canada by Random House of Canada Limited, Toronto, Penguin Random House Companies. Pictureback, Random House, and the Random House colophon are registered trademarks of Random House LLC.

ISBN 978-0-553-50870-3

randomhousekids.com   www.thomasandfriends.com

MANUFACTURED IN CHINA 10 9 8 7 6 5 4 3 2

HiT entertainment